NIMBY AND BUBBLES

Written
by
Christina Fragola

Illustrated
by
Marta Prior

© 2015 Christina Fragola
Illustrations © 2015 Marta Prior

All Rights Reserved.

No part of this publication may be reproduced, stored in a retrieval system, or transmitted, in any form or by any means, electronic, mechanical, photocopying, recording, or otherwise, without the written permission of the author.

First published by Dog Ear Publishing
4011 Vincennes Rd
Indianapolis, IN 46268
www.dogearpublishing.net

ISBN: 978-1-4575-3904-6

This book is printed on acid-free paper.

This book is a work of fiction. Places, events, and situations in this book are purely fictional and any resemblance to actual persons, living or dead, is coincidental.

Printed in the United States of America

Nimby walked slowly into the forest with tears in his young porcupine eyes.

"I can't believe this is happening to me!" he cried out loud, looking up at the sky.

Just moments before, Nimby had been surrounded by a group of young porcupines taunting and jeering at him. Nimby began to walk faster into the woods, but he couldn't get their words out of his head: "You are no one!!!" and, "What good are you if you can't fight like the rest of us!!!"

For it was true, Nimby could not fight like the rest of them. The rest of the porcupines could raise their quills until they roared, and lash out with their tails until they soared. When it came time for him to protect himself or others, Nimby's sleek black quills would not budge.

"I'm going to run away and never come back!!! Yeah, I'll show them! I can make it on my own. I don't need anybody!" His spirits began to brighten and he even smiled a little, but as he walked further into the forest he wondered if he was so happy on his own, why was he feeling so sad?

Moments later, Nimby heard someone crying. "Boo hoo hoo," and again, "Waaaaaah, boo hoo." He leaned into the babbling brook wondering if it had come from there. The crying grew louder:

"BOO HOO HOO... Waaaaaaaaa!"

Nimby said, "Hello! Who is there? Is that you crying, babbling brook? Please call out... tell me who you are... Hello...

who are…" Nimby was suddenly interrupted by a tiny indignant voice,

"If you would stop shouting (sniffle sniffle), I will tell you (sniffle sniffle)!"

"Oh," said Nimby, becoming very quiet. He walked toward the brook and out from under a bush flew a little bumblebee.

"Well hello!" exclaimed Nimby, startled. "My name is Nimby Porcupine. What's your name, and why, yes, why are you crying?"

The bumblebee sniffled a bit more. "My name is Bubbles, and I don't know why I was crying."

"You don't know?" asked Nimby. "You don't know??? Well maybe I can help you. What are you doing out here all by yourself?"

"Well," said Bubbles, "I sort of ran away from home. You see, the other bees were making fun of me and calling me names. I'm different from them. They can sting, but I can't, and they say I'm no good. Oh, boo hoo hoo!!!"

"Oh, how sad!" cried Nimby, and suddenly Nimby burst into tears.

"Why are *you* crying, Nimby-Head?" asked Bubbles through sniffles.

"Because they make fun of me, too! And don't call me Nimby-Head, Boobles!"

"Hey, don't call me Boobles!" Bubbles cried out.

"Oh, my goodness," Nimby realized though his tears, "now we're making fun of each other! We can't do that. But what can we do? We have to stick together and figure out what we should do! We have to find a way to get you a stinger, and I need to find out how to make my quills roar and my tail soar like the others or we will be nobodies! We can't protect any one! What shall we do??? What shall we do? Help! Help! Help!"

"Nimby! Get a grip!!!" Bubbles interrupted. "Gee Whiz!!! Shouting about it is definitely not going to help. Hmmmmmmm. Let's see... Why don't we just try to have a wee bit of fun and maybe we'll think of something."

"Good idea, Bubbles! You are so smart!" Nimby said with awe.

And off they went across the brook and through the trees. Nimby got stuck in the bushes and Bubbles helped him out. Bubbles bumped into a tree and Nimby picked her up.

As the sky grew dark and the sun began to set, Nimby and Bubbles began to feel a little sleepy and a little sad. It was the first time either of them had been away from home. Soon they discovered a big tree, curled up together and fell asleep.

~~~~~~~~~~~~~

As the birds chirped and the sun began to rise, Bubbles opened her eyes and at first was not sure where she was. Still sleepy, she heard mumbling next to her and realized she was somewhere in the woods with her new friend Nimby.

"No, no don't," Nimby was mumbling in his sleep.

Bubbles nudged him. "Wake up. Wake up!"

Nimby woke up startled.

"Hey! I had a dream! I was lost in the woods and I didn't know where I was. I shouted 'pleh,' but didn't know what it meant. There was a mirror, and so I looked in the mirror and the words were coming out of my mouth: 'pleh, pleh, pleh! But in the mirror I saw that it spelled 'help' backwards!"

Bubbles was listening intently and exclaimed, "Wow Nimby, you were calling out for help!"

"No I wasn't!" Nimby stamped his feet. "It was help spelled backwards."

"Hmmmmm," said Bubbles, "I get it! You just look in the mirror to see it spelled right! Hee hee! Pleh! Pleh! Pleh!"

"Pleh!" they both shouted together.

"Interesting dream," a low soft voice said out of nowhere.

"Hey, who said that?" cried Nimby.

Bubbles giggled, as she tended to do when she got nervous and added, "Yes, who said that?"

"Very interesting dream," said the voice again, louder and lower.

They looked around and at the same time they both looked up to discover two large, warm eyes staring down at them.

"Welcome," they heard a soft deep voice say.

"Hey! Who are you?" Nimby shouted.

"I am Willow, little one," she answered.

"Hey! Don't call me little one. What is going on here?" asked Nimby.

The large weeping willow opened her branches as if stretched out to greet them.

"Forgive me, but I have been watching you sleep. You both seem to have a lot on your minds. Troubled is a word that comes to mind. Is there something I can help you with?"

"Well yes...," Bubbles started to say when she was interrupted by Nimby, who stated, "No! Don't tell her anything. She can't help us. She'll just make fun of us and tell us to go home. We'll figure it out for ourselves. We can learn to fight; we can!!!"

And the weeping willow responded, "Who tells you that you must learn to fight, young porcupine?" Her branches were long and swaying in the wind.

"Bubbles needs to learn to sting and I need to learn to attack with my beautiful black quills," Nimby insisted.

"Why do you need to hurt others? Who will you sting, Bubbles? Who will you prickle, Nimby? I saw you off in the distance before you fell asleep under my branches, and you both looked so happy, singing and dancing and helping each other out. What other journey could there possibly be, little ones?" Willow waited for a response.

Nimby puffed up his cheeks and shouted, "I told you not to call us little ones! And you can't tell us what to do, either! What do you know anyway? It's not all just singing and dancing. We are going now, so LEAVE US ALONE!!!"

"Come on, Bubbles!"

And off they went.

They walked in silence for a while and then Bubbles finally said, "Maybe you were a bit hard on Willow. She seemed so smart and all."

"No Bubbles, she won't understand. We need to be able to fit in. Do you really want to get made fun of all the time?"

Bubbles shook her head no.

"I didn't think so," said Nimby.

They walked on in silence, unsure where they were going and suddenly not too sure why they were going anywhere. Everywhere they seemed to be hearing, "You have to fit in. You have to fit in." The birds were chirping it and the leaves were whispering it. What were they going to do next? They walked on.

Big Hair

"Help! Help! Help!"

They both seemed to hear it at the same time.

"Where is that coming from?" Nimby asked Bubbles.

"HELP! HELP! HELP!"

The voice became louder and Bubbles noticed it was over by the cave.

"Hurry, over this way," said Bubbles.

They ran over to the cave and saw three young porcupines tied to a rock in front of the cave entrance.

Nimby asked, "What is going on? What are you doing here? Who did this? Oh, what are we going to do? What..."

"Please sir," began one of the porcupines meekly, "if you would stop talking I could explain..."

"Don't mind Nimby," Bubbles giggled, "he gets a little overexcited sometimes."

"Oh yes, I guess I do," Nimby giggled, then caught himself and stated, "but this is no laughing matter!"

"No, it is not," cried one of the other porcupines. "We were playing near the cave, battling with our quills and teasing the other animals, when all of a sudden this big huge hairy monster jumped out of nowhere!" The porcupine began to cry.

The third porcupine chimed in, stating, "Yes, and now here we are and he tied us up and we don't know what he's going to do!"

"Oh dear," said Nimby. "How can we help? You see, Bubbles and I, well, we can't… we don't … my quills won't budge…"

Bubbles then interrupted, looking quite sad, and said, "And me, I can't sting anyone."

The first porcupine spoke up, "No, you don't understand. Those things wouldn't help anyway. This hairy-thing is BIG... I tell you he's VERY BIG. You'll have to outsmart him, I think. Yes, that's it. Outsmart him."

Porcupine number two then added, "It's the only way."

"Hmmmmmm…" Bubbles was thinking, but before she could speak a voice bellowed out from the cave, "HA! YOU THINK YOU CAN OUTSMART ME?"

"Aaaaccckkk!!!" they all shouted and attempted to huddle together.

Seconds later, the hairy monster came out of the cave with his arms stretched out so wide they could cover the horizon. And he was so tall that his head almost touched the sky. And he was hairy. Very hairy.

Nimby was the first to speak. "Oh, my goodness. Oh, my gosh. What is this? What are we to do? Oh dear, what..."

"Nimby, please quiet down," Bubbles interrupted. "We have to remain calm."

The two of them stared up at the monster, who stared down at them scowling, "WHO DO YOU THINK YOU ARE???" he bellowed.

Bubbles grew bold all of a sudden knowing it was she who had to take charge. "We don't *think* we are anybody. We *know* who we are!"

"HA, HA, HA," the monster laughed, "a toughie, are you?"

Bubbles replied, "Yes, I am tough and I don't like that you've tied up these porcupines."

"Well, isn't that just too bad, cause I may tie you up and your buddy there, too, and then we'll see how tough you are. Or I may just throw you off the mountain. HA!!!"

The monster stepped towards them. The ground shook. Bubbles thought he was about to bare his big sharp teeth. She was a little scared, but kept thinking, *I have to outsmart him. I just have to.* Bubbles looked him in the eye and said, "If I were a dentist I would take out your teeth, you BIG BULLY!!!"

All of a sudden the monster looked very sad. He opened his mouth and stated, "Oh, but look!" He opened his mouth wider. "I don't have any teeth!"

And then the big bully hairy monster sat down, put his hands on his head and began to cry. And cry. And cry. Somehow, watching those tears made everybody sad for the monster.

"Awww," said Nimby, "don't cry mister. Please don't cry. We understand. In fact, if you weren't so mean to us, we might like you."

"Yes, please don't cry," begged Bubbles. "I guess you are so mean because you have no teeth and you have to prove you are tough."

The monster looked up, his face brightening. "Maybe you are right! And yet you think you like me? You really like me?" he sniffled.

Bubbles hesitated and said, "Well, two seconds ago you were going to throw us over the mountain."

"Oh, I never would have done that. I am so sorry. You two have helped me see the light. Yes, I saw the light! Yippee! Yahoo! I saw the light!!!" The monster looked up and shook his gigantic hands in the air.

Bubbles began to giggle. "Well ok, I do like you, mister. Come on, Nimby, what about you?"

"Oooh, well," Nimby answered, smiling, "of course I do!"

They all laughed together and began to dance a jig.

"Excuse me," interrupted Porcupine number one. "I hate to interrupt your little party, but, well, we would really appreciate it if someone would untie us!"

The three jig dancers stopped and stared at the three porcupines.

"Whoops!" they all said in unison and giggled a little. The monster untied them and they ran off with glee.

"And stop teasing the animals!" Nimby yelled after them.

After the porcupines left, Bubbles looked up at the hairy monster, realizing she didn't know his name. "What is your name anyway," she asked.

"My name? My name is Bamboo."

"Bamboo???" Nimby and Bubbles stated together. "Well, if you say so." They both giggled at his funny name.

Bubbles and Nimby knew it was time to go. They looked at each other, pleased about the way their day was going. And it was not just because they saved the porcupines. They had made a new friend. They had helped him see that being mean was not the answer to his problems, and that he could have no teeth and still have friends.

Nimby and Bubbles were getting ready to continue their journey. Bamboo knew they had to leave, but looked sad.

Bubbles noticed this and told him, "Don't worry, Bamboo, we'll be back. In fact, we'll come tomorrow for a picnic, right Nimby?"

"Right indeed!" shouted Nimby.

Bamboo's eyes lit up and he exclaimed, "You will? You promise? You promise? Oh, will you really...?"

"Get a grip, Bamboo. Yes, we promise!" exclaimed Bubbles.

"Ok, ok," laughed Bamboo.

Bamboo had a huge toothless smile on his face as he waved good-bye to his new friends. Nimby and Bubbles waved back as they set off into the forest to continue their journey.

The Teeth

Nimby and Bubbles walked through the forest and soon they came across a pond. The pond was still and quiet with no signs of life.

At the sight of the pond Nimby exclaimed, "This is strange. I have never seen anything like it!" He looked across the pond wondering where all of the frogs and ducks were.

"What do you mean, Nimby? You've never seen a pond before?" asked Bubbles.

"No silly, of course I've seen a pond. But take a look. This one is different."

Bubbles looked across the pond and saw what Nimby was talking about. "Where is everybody!?" she exclaimed. "I don't see any ducks… no frogs… I don't even see any fish!" Bubbles leaned over and looked into the pond. All she could see was her reflection. "Hmmm," she said, "it is strange!"

"Very strange indeed!" added Nimby. "What should we do? We have to figure this out. I mean, where did everybody go? What could have happened? Where can they be? Huh, Bubbles… what should…"

"Nimby please!" Bubbles interrupted. "I am trying to think and I can't hear myself think with you babbling on and on."

"Ok," said Nimby, "I'll keep quiet, but please think hard!!!"

And Bubbles did. She thought and thought and thought, and then stated, "Well Nimby, I have no idea what could have happened. We must investigate!"

And off they went, walking around the pond and looking for clues. Soon, they heard something rustling in the bushes near the side of the pond.

"Who goes there?" shouted Nimby. The rustling in the bushes stopped, but there was no answer.

"Who goes there, I said," repeated Nimby.

Complete silence.

Nimby and Bubbles slowly moved closer to where the noise had been coming from. They were tiptoeing forward when all of a sudden an alligator came running out of the bushes with his mouth wide open. And he had teeth. A lot of teeth. A lot of teeth indeed.

"Aaaccckkk!!!" Nimby and Bubbles screamed as they ran away from the ferocious mouth.

The alligator moved towards them with his mouth partly shut so it looked as though he was smirking at them. And then he shouted, "Who do you think you are, hanging around my pond?"

Nimby and Bubbles were so frightened that they could not answer.

"DID YOU HEAR WHAT I SAID?!" the toothy alligator shouted even louder.

All of a sudden, Bubbles grew bold. "No, we didn't hear what you said, you big goofy guy!"

"What did you call me?" the alligator growled.

"You heard me," snapped Bubbles.

"Yeah, you heard Bubbles," Nimby chimed in, also growing bold.

"Somebody named Bubbles is talking back to me, O' Mighty Alley-Alligator?"

"Yes, O Mighty-what-ever your name is," answered Bubbles. "And you know what? I want to know what is going on around here. Where is everybody?"

The alligator looked at them, and this time it was clear that he was smirking at them, and he shouted, "I ate them! I ate them all!!! AH, HA, HA, HA, HA, HA!!!" he laughed.

"I'm not quite sure what is so funny, Mr. Alley," stated Bubbles.

And Nimby added, "Yes, Mr. Alley, what is so funny?"

"HA!" Alley snorted. "HA, HA, HA!!! I'll tell you what is so funny. I will, I will, I will, oh yes, I will, I..."

"Would you just tell us for crying out loud!" interrupted Bubbles.

Alley looked startled, as if Bubbles had woken him up from a trance. "Ok, I will, I, uh will." Alley paused, about to explain and then all of a sudden he looked sad, as if he realized that what he was about to say wasn't so funny after all. He opened his mouth to say something and instead he began to shed a tear, and then another tear, and then another, and soon he was shedding very large crocodile tears.

"I can't help but cry," he sobbed. "I cry all of the time, these big crocodile tears, and I am an alligator! I am O' Mighty Alley-Alligator, and yet I shed these big crocodile tears! One day when I was feeling so sad, I just ate everything in the pond one by one. And I felt mighty! I did not shed one tear! And now you two come along and I realize that I have done wrong! Oh, boo hoo hoo, what have I done? What have I done???" and Alley began to cry even harder.

"Don't cry, Mr. Alley, we'll help you," said Bubbles, dodging his tears so she wouldn't drown.

"Yes, we'll help you," added Nimby. "But how?"

Nimby looked at Bubbles and realized that she already had her thinking cap on. "Oooh, I better keep quiet, Bubbles is thinking," he muttered to himself.

Alley and Nimby waited patiently as they stared at Bubbles.

Soon Bubbles shouted, "I've got it!!! By gosh, by golly, I've got it!!!

"Got what, got what???" cried Nimby and Alley at the same time.

"Open your mouth, Alley," Bubbles ordered sternly.

Alley followed the order, no questions asked.

"And keep it open," added Bubbles.

And with that, Bubbles flew into Alley's mouth.

"Oh no!!!" screamed Nimby. "Don't leave me, Bubbles, please don't leave me! Bubbles please!!! Please…"

Soon he heard Bubbles' far-away voice, "Don't worry, Nimby, I'll be baaaaaccckkkk……."

So Nimby waited. And he waited. He stared at Alley, whose mouth was as wide as it could be. Soon he heard Bubbles far-away voice again: "Follow me everybody, follow meeeeeee…"

And a moment later, first came Bubbles, then came a frog hopping and a duck quacking, and another duck quacking and two more frogs hopping, and three birds chirping, and two flies, and a polliwog!

Alley closed his mouth and stared in awe at Bubbles and Nimby and the marching, chirping, quacking, hopping whole bunch of them!

Alley cried out with glee, and then stated, "Oh, thank you sooooooo much! By saving them, you saved me!" Alley then began to break into song, repeating over and over, "by saving them, you saved me; by saving them, you saved me…"

The three of them watched as the group marched into the pond laughing and cheering. One solitary crocodile tear fell as Alley saw how happy everybody was, but Alley didn't mind; he liked it.

They all smiled at each other. Dancing a jig seemed out of the question, but they had to say good-bye. Nimby and Bubbles knew it was time to move on.

"I know!!!" shouted Nimby before they walked away. "Let's invite Alley to the picnic!"

"Picnic!?" shouted Alley. "Picnic!!!" he shouted again. "I love picnics! Can I really come?"

"Of course you can, silly," answered Bubbles. "That is what Nimby is saying!"

"Hooray!" Alley exclaimed.

"Hooray!!!" all three of them shouted together.

Nimby and Bubbles then waved good-bye and walked on through the forest.

RED

They walked on unsure of where they would go next. Suddenly, as Nimby started to speak, what appeared to be a bright red ball came bouncing towards them!

"Aaaccckkk!!!" they both screamed, and ran out of the way. Nimby dove on the ground covering Bubbles.

"What in the world!!!?" cried Nimby. "What in the blippity blip world was that!?"

As they stood up the red ball came out of nowhere again and bounced hard right in front of them... BOUNCE, BOUNCE, BOUNCE!!!

As the ball came down they heard a voice squealing, "You can see me, but I see you first!!!" BOUNCE! And then louder, "HA! HA! HA! YOU CAN SEE ME, BUT I SEE YOU FIRST!" Bounce! Bounce! BOUNCE!!!

Nimby and Bubbles scrambled to get out of the way. *This can't be!* thought Bubbles. *It just can't be!* As scared as she and Nimby were, Bubbles began to get angry at the way this ball was treating them. Very angry indeed.

Bubbles could not hold back any longer, "Cut it out you... you, Beast!!!" she shouted.

The bouncing ball stopped and then Bubbles heard laughter. The ball was behind the bushes laughing away. "That is funny, bumble bee, you bumbley bee! But you cannot see me, me, me!!!"

Bubbles responded, "Yes we *can* see you and we *don't* like what we see, you meanie!!!"

Nimby then became braver and added, "Yeah, you meanie!!! We don't like it!!!"

Suddenly the ball bounced out of the bushes and came to a halt with a little bounce. The bright red ball then appeared to come to life right before their eyes, and they saw with surprise that it wasn't a red ball after all. It was a silly, goofy, bright red lizard!"

Nimby giggled.

"Laugh all you want," the lizard exclaimed. "I am Leo the Lizard and you can't touch me!"

At this, Bubbles giggled and stated, "Ooooh, you are so cool! So cool, red stuff! You're so bright you make my cheeks turn red!!! You're as bright as cinnamon candy!! You're as bright as Santa's red suit. You're as bright as an apple..."

Nimby then interrupted, stating, "Yeah, a granny apple!"

Bubbles looked at Nimby and laughed. "You're so silly, Nimby. Granny apples aren't red!!! They're green!!!"

Nimby and Bubbles began to giggle and giggle. "Hee, hee, hee, that's so funny! Hee, hee, hee…"

"STOP IT!!!" shouted the suddenly serious Leo at the two giggling animals. "Stop it, stop it, stop it!!!" And then the bouncy, loud, loquacious lizard named Leo sat down and began to cry.

"Oh dear," exclaimed Nimby when he saw the lizard crying, "what is up with this forest? So many tears! Oh dear, oh dear, oh dear!"

"Oh dear, indeed," Bubbles added. "We made fun of him and now he is crying." Bubbles looked at Leo and stated, "We're sorry. We didn't mean to make you cry."

"No, we didn't," added Nimby.

Leo looked up, still sniffling. "No, you were right to make fun of me. I am so red and bright. None of the other lizards look like me. They're all green. They can hide in the woods and be safe and protect themselves, and look out for each other. Me? I'm an eye sore. I look funny and I'm different… oh, boo hoo hoo!" Leo began to cry again.

Bubbles was the first to speak, "Oh don't be silly. We made fun of you because you were mean to us. In fact we think you are dazzling! Don't we Nimby?"

"Oh yes," Nimby replied, "we do. We do indeed!"

When the lizard heard this, and as red as he already was, he blushed even redder and stated, "You really think I'm dazzling?"

"Yes! In fact, we'd love it if you would come to our picnic tomorrow. Would you like that?" asked Bubbles.

"Would I ever!" exclaimed Leo. "I've been mean and rotten for so long… what a waste! A picnic! I can hardly wait!" And he smiled a huge, bright red lizard smile and bounced a little jig.

"Hooray!" shouted Nimby. "Hooray, hooray, hooray!" Nimby then began to twirl around. Leo and Bubbles watched him go round and round.

"Ok, Nimby!" Bubbles had to interrupt for it was time to end their journey. It was time to move on. Nimby stopped twirling. He felt dizzy but happy. He and Bubbles waved good-bye to the bright red lizard named Leo.

"See you tomorrow!" Leo called after them as he waved and watched them walk happily away.

Willow

As they moved through the forest they were heading in a direction they had already been. Somehow they both knew that before they finished their journey they had to return to see Willow. When they finally got there, Willow's eyes were closed. Nimby and Bubbles stared at her beautiful face and didn't know what to say. It looked as if she were napping and they were afraid to wake her up.

"No, I'm just resting," she explained, opening her eyes and talking to them as if she could read their thoughts. "I thought that maybe you'd be back."

Nimby and Bubbles stared at Willow and remained silent until Bubbles spoke. "Yes, we are back. We've had quite a day, you know." She paused. "We've met all sorts of characters." She stopped talking, still staring at Willow.

Nimby chimed in, "We did indeed. All sorts. Indeed!"

Bubbles continued, "This morning seems so far away! But we remember what you said to us about why we thought we had to fight. Well, you were right! We were stuck on the wrong things. We thought we were oddballs! Weirdos. We thought…"

"But we are oddballs! We are weird!" Nimby interrupted.

Bubbles had to disagree. "I am no oddball. I am Bubbles!"

Willow shared her thoughts and stated, "Oddballs are the fruit of the earth, Bubbles. Oddballs are unique, fun and quirky."

"Quirky?" Bubbles asked.

"Strange, but cool. Idiosyncratic," said Willow.

"Well, that is a big word!" giggled Bubbles.

Nimby chimed in again. "Bubbles, we are strange, but cool! We are idiostinkcractic!"

"It's idiosyncratic, Nimby!"

"Oh, who cares! We are what we are! Why would we want to blend in when we can stand out. Right Bubbles!?"

"Right Nimby!" Bubbles agreed.

Nimby added, "And we met all sorts of oddballs on our journey!"

Bubbles began to get excited and added, "That's right! We did and we are going on a picnic! And we are going to have fun!" Bubbles burst into song:

"We's a goin. Together. On a picnic. What's the weather? We's a goin together. On a picnic. Don't care bout the weather. We's a goin…" Bubbles seemed lost in a trance singing.

"Gee Bubbles, where did you go?" Nimby interrupted.

Willow spoke. "Bubbles is just very excited. I can see that she sings when she is happy. Just remember, being different brought you two together, and all the other animals you met on your journey."

Bubbles stopped singing and said to Willow, "And we met you, too, Willow!"

"Yeah, that's right," added Nimby, "and we aren't yelling at you no more!" Nimby giggled a little thinking about when he had first met Willow.

"Great to meet you both, Bubs and Nimbs," said Willow. "So what else?"

"Hey, don't call us Bubs and Nimbs, hee, hee," Nimby exclaimed.

"So sorry. I just can't help myself. You look so cute and happy, Nimby and Bubbles," said Willow. "Come visit anytime!"

"Hooray!" shouted Nimby and Bubbles at the same time.

Everyone was very happy! Nimby and Bubbles did their final jig for the day, realizing it was time to go home. They walked towards home, waving good-bye to Willow. Willow waved back.

"Look," exclaimed Nimby pointing at Willow, "it looks like Willow's branches are blowing in the wind!"

Bubbles giggled and stated, "No silly, she is waving good-bye to us!"

"Oh, whoops, who knew?" Nimby giggled.

As they walked on they realized it was time for them to part. They both seemed a little sad, but knew that tomorrow was the start of a brand new day, and tomorrow was the picnic!!!

"Yahoo! We go on the picnic tomorrow," exclaimed Nimby.

"Yes we do!" stated Bubbles.

"So, see you tomorrow," they both stated at the same time.

"Pleh," added Nimby as he turned to go home.

"Bless you," said Bubbles.

Nimby giggled, "I didn't sneeze, I said pleh! Pleh, pleh, pleh!"

Bubbles giggled, "Pleh-choo!!"

They giggled some more and then hugged good-bye. They would meet tomorrow where they started today, by the bush near the babbling brook. As they walked their separate ways, both began singing their new song:

"We's a goin. Together. On a picnic. What's the weather? We's a goin together…"

Nimby was then heard muttering, "I can't wait. Indeed I can't. Indeedy-do."

The End